The Cavernous Imp Castle
Bellua

Immie Imp
The hole in the second root on the
The Imp Oak
Bellua

D0965214

Immie,

My excellent plan has begun. I have seized a magical power from a pitiful dragon – the first of many creatures! I WILL become the supreme ruler of the entire Kingdom of Bellua. Once I've collected enough powers, no one will be able to stop me – not even a vile Guardian.

I am sending YOU, Immie, to stop the new Guardian from curing the creatures of Bellua. There must be no happiness in Bellua. All must fear me! If you fail in your task, the Guardian will destroy my rule of misery and despair.

The new Guardian is just a wimpy girl so your task will be easy, even for you. Do not fail me, imp. You must NOT let her threaten the advance of the mighty Ivar.

Signed,

King Ivar

All Mighty, All Powerful, Supreme
(and handsome) King of the Imps

Read all the adventures of

THE DRAGON'S SONG

THE UNICORN'S HORN

THE FAIRY'S WING

THE MERMAID'S TAIL

Hattie B Magical Vet

The Dragon's Song

CLAIRE TAYLOR-SMITH

Illustrated by Lorena Alvarez

PUFFIN

PUFFIN BOOKS

Published by the Penguin Group
Penguin Books Ltd, 80 Strand, London WC2R ORL, England
Penguin Group (USA) Inc., 375 Hudson Street, New York, New York 10014, USA
Penguin Group (Canada), 90 Eglinton Avenue East, Suite 700, Toronto, Ontario, Canada M4P 2Y3
(a division of Pearson Penguin Canada Inc.)
Penguin Ireland, 25 St Stephen's Green, Dublin 2, Ireland (a division of Penguin Books Ltd)
Penguin Group (Australia), 707 Collins Street, Melbourne, Victoria 3008, Australia
(a division of Pearson Australia Group Pty Ltd)
Penguin Books India Pvt Ltd, 11 Community Centre, Panchsheel Park, New Delhi – 110 017, India
Penguin Group (NZ), 67 Apollo Drive, Rosedale, Auckland 0632, New Zealand
(a division of Pearson New Zealand Ltd)
Penguin Books (South Africa) (Pty) Ltd, Block D, Rosebank Office Park,
181 Jan Smuts Avenue, Parktown North, Gauteng 2193, South Africa

Penguin Books Ltd, Registered Offices: 80 Strand, London WC2R ORL, England

puffinbooks.com

First published 2014
001

Text and illustrations copyright © Penguin Books Ltd, 2014
Story concept originated by Mums Creative Content Ltd
Illustrations by Lorena Alvarez
With thanks to Claire Baker
All rights reserved

The moral right of the copyright holders and illustrator has been asserted

Set in 14.5/24pt Bembo Book MT Std
Typeset by Jouve (UK), Milton Keynes
Printed in Great Britain by Clays Ltd, St Ives plc

British Library Cataloguing in Publication Data
A CIP catalogue record for this book is available from the British Library

ISBN: 978-0-141-34462-1

www.greenpenguin.co.uk

MIX
Paper from
responsible sources
FSC® C018179

Penguin Books is committed to a sustainable
future for our business, our readers and our planet.
This book is made from Forest Stewardship
Council™ certified paper.

Love always to

Harriet (the original Hattie),

Annie, Natascha and Zac

xxx

Winter
Mountains

Cave

Valley
of the
Guardians

Pixie
Park

Elf
Avenue

Dragon's
Valley

Unicorn
Meadows

Silvery Stream

Enchanted
Orchard

Contents

The Worst Birthday Ever

It was eight o'clock on a sunny Saturday morning in March. Hattie Bright leapt out of bed, pulled on her Dalmatian-patterned dressing-gown and stepped into her bunny-shaped slippers.

I can't believe I'm ten today! she thought.

Bursting with excitement, Hattie remembered the birthday sleepover she and her best friend

Chloe had arranged for that night. Then there were the animal-themed presents she guessed would be waiting for her downstairs! Hattie's family and friends knew that she *loved* animals and they always chose gifts with cute cats or dogs on them – or ponies, or rabbits, or just about any other animal anyone could think of. Hattie adored them all.

Hattie bounded down the stairs, but when she burst into the living room it looked just the same as when she had gone to bed the night before. There were no presents piled up by the old Victorian fireplace and none heaped on the sofa either. All she could see on the coffee table were two empty mugs from last night.

Hattie couldn't believe it! No birthday presents and – even worse – she could see her parents in the hall, putting on their coats and getting ready to go to work at their vet's practice in town.

'Are you and Dad both going to work, Mum?' asked Hattie, who had hoped that at least one of them might have taken the day off for her birthday. Hattie's mum nodded as she tied a brightly patterned silk scarf round her neck. 'B-but don't you know what day it is?' added Hattie, not believing her own parents could have forgotten it was her birthday.

'Yes, of course,' replied Mum. 'It's Saturday.

What a silly question! Now, we're going to be really late for our first patient if we don't get a move on. We should be home before lunchtime, though, and Peter's in his room if you need him.'

'B-but –' Hattie stammered in protest. She knew that Peter, her grumpy teenage brother, wasn't likely to even get up by lunchtime, let alone wish her a happy birthday.

'But nothing, young lady,' interrupted Mum. 'We really had better get going. So see you just after twelve. Bye!'

And, with that, Mum and Dad swept out of the house. The front door slammed and Hattie found herself standing alone in the hall, convinced that this was going to be her worst birthday *ever*.

Back in the living room, Hattie slumped in an armchair with the phone, ready to call

Chloe and tell her how her birthday had got off to such a terrible start. But after a couple of rings Chloe's mum answered. She told Hattie that Chloe wasn't at home because she had spent last night at her cousin's house and was almost certainly going to stay there for the whole weekend. Hattie was devastated as she thought, *What about our sleepover plans?*

'I'm sure Chloe will tell you all about it back at school on Monday morning,' added Chloe's mum in a cheery voice. 'Bye for now, Hattie – have a lovely weekend!'

As Hattie said goodbye in a slightly shaky voice, she thought she heard a muffled giggle coming down the phone – a giggle that sounded very much like it might have come from Chloe herself.

Hattie gasped and slammed down the phone with tears pricking in her eyes. Was Chloe actually at home after all? Was she there with some other friends when it was Hattie's birthday? The tears started pouring down Hattie's cheeks and dripping on to her dressing-gown collar. This definitely was the worst birthday *ever* – Chloe was meant to be her best friend!

Feeling really upset that Chloe could treat her so badly, Hattie ran upstairs and grabbed the butterfly writing set that Grandma had bought her last Christmas. She sat down at her small wooden desk and rummaged in her kitten pencil case for a pen before furiously scribbling down how she felt:

Dear Chloe,

I thought it was bad enough when my mum and dad forgot my birthday, but now it looks like you have too! Your mum says you probably won't be here for my birthday sleepover either, even after we spent all that time planning the midnight feast and which DVD we were going to watch. I thought you

*were my best friend, but a best friend wouldn't
forget something <u>this</u> important, so maybe we
just can't be friends any more.*

Your ex-best friend,
Hattie

She folded the letter and angrily pushed it into an
envelope. That would show Chloe! Hattie was
never going to trust her, or anyone, again – ever.

Before writing Chloe's name on the envelope,
Hattie paused just for a moment, feeling horrible.
Did she *really* want to send this? Could Chloe
really have done this to her? Then Hattie
remembered the giggle at the other end of the

phone. Yes, she *was* going to send the letter. She wanted Chloe to know how upset she was that her best friend had let her down. Hattie felt so hurt that she didn't even care when a tear fell on to the ink, turning Chloe's name into a smudgy mess.

She stomped back downstairs, adding the envelope to a pile of her mum's letters that were on the kitchen table, waiting to be posted when she got home.

Still sniffing tearfully, Hattie looked at the big round clock that hung just above the cooker. It wasn't even nine o'clock yet, so there was a whole morning to fill when she should have been enjoying all her birthday presents. She couldn't believe that *everyone* had let her down, not just her best friend but her mum and dad too! Hattie was just thinking about dragging her duvet downstairs and curling up on the sofa with a magazine when she heard someone knocking at the front door. *Knock, knock.* There it was again.

'Get that, will you, Hattie!' Peter bellowed down the stairs.

Hattie humphed. So Peter was awake after all, but just too lazy to come down and open the door – or wish her a happy birthday, for that matter.

She opened the door and peered out, but there was nobody there. *How strange!*

She was about to close it when something
on the doorstep caught her eye. A little warily,
Hattie bent down to take a closer look.

A Very Mysterious Gift

A parcel sat on the doorstep, wrapped tightly in old-fashioned brown paper and held together with both brown tape and string. Hattie's name and address were written in one corner in elaborate curly writing. In the opposite corner was a very unusual stamp, with all the colours of the rainbow swirled together on it and edges that sparkled brightly. Hattie had never even heard of the country printed along its bottom edge. She couldn't imagine who had sent it.

As she reached down to see if the parcel held any further clues, a sickly sweet voice sailed across the front garden.

'Hey, Hattie, nice dressing-gown – black and white, just like your hair!'

Hattie looked up to see Victoria Frost standing by the garden gate, looking perfect as usual, in a pink tutu and matching ballet cardigan. Her blonde hair was pulled into a neatly pinned bun. Standing beside Victoria were her two identically dressed friends, Jodie and Louisa, who, like Victoria, were in Hattie's class at school. And they were just as mean, always laughing at Victoria's spiteful jokes. Hattie ran her hand anxiously through her long dark hair, twisting her distinctive white streak round her fingers. Victoria was often mean about Hattie's hair. Hattie's mum and dad said her unusual white streak made her special, and Hattie thought so too. But Victoria Frost always had a way of making Hattie feel bad about herself.

'Having a birthday lie-in, were you?' continued Victoria with a sneer. 'It *is* your birthday today, isn't it? Only it's really hard to tell. On my birthday my parents had over a hundred pink balloons in our front garden so that *everyone* knew it was my special day.'

Hattie watched as Victoria made a great

show of looking around Hattie's front garden,
sniggering at the sparse rose bushes, which
were clearly no substitute for pink balloons.
Jodie and Louisa laughed nastily behind her.

Hattie felt her face turn bright red with

embarrassment before Victoria decided to leave her alone.

She swept off in the direction of the village green, turning away from the gate with a dramatic flourish. 'Better get off to dance class,' she called, beckoning the other girls to follow. 'We don't want to keep Hattie from her *birthday* celebrations, do we, girls?'

And, with a flash of pink netting and perfect hair, all three girls strutted off down the road, leaving Hattie to flee into the house with the parcel, slamming the door shut behind her.

Back inside, and still clutching the parcel, Hattie ran straight upstairs and threw herself on to her bed, burying her face in the pillow as her eyes filled with tears again. She wished Victoria Frost's comments didn't always upset her so much, but she was just so horrid! Could this birthday get any worse?

Hattie sighed, shifting her head on the now tear-dampened pillowcase. She peered out of one eye at the strange parcel next to her. She had been really excited until Victoria had ruined the moment. Who could have sent it? Surely not Victoria! Whoever it was from, Hattie decided that after such a terrible morning she had nothing to lose by opening it.

She sat up and started to unpick the knots in the string that held it together.

The parcel had been wrapped and tied very tightly – Hattie's fingers were quite sore after undoing all the string. Someone had clearly taken a lot of time and care to make sure it would be a lot of trouble for anyone to open. She wondered what on earth it could hold.

Hattie peeled open the brown paper. The rich and musty smell of old leather wafted up. Inside was what seemed to be an ancient leather bag – the sort a vet might have used many years ago. It was a darkish-brown colour, creased and scuffed as though it had been well used. Hattie's first thought was to open it and look inside, but when she tried she realized it was locked.

What a strange present, thought Hattie, feeling slightly disappointed.

Turning the bag round in her hands, she examined it from every angle before placing it on the floor beside her. As she did so, Hattie's tummy flipped with nervous excitement – because there, nestled in the discarded brown paper, was something small and glittery. Carefully picking it up, she saw it was a pretty silver bracelet with a star-shaped crystal charm hanging from it. It was beautiful, exactly the sort of thing Hattie liked to wear – and something about it felt strangely familiar.

Hattie rummaged through the paper again to look for a note, but there was nothing. She had no way of knowing who had sent her these two very different presents. She couldn't imagine when she would ever need to use the vet's bag, but as she slipped the bracelet on to her wrist she couldn't help feeling a little better that at least *someone* had remembered it was her birthday today.

It was nearly lunchtime when Hattie had finally got dressed and was sprawled out lazily on her unmade bed. She had an empty bag of crisps beside her, having munched through them while watching two DVDs in a row all by herself. Hattie had shouted through Peter's closed door to see if he'd wanted to join her, but he'd just grunted some reply about animal films being 'girly' without even coming out of his room.

Every so often Hattie had glanced down at her new bracelet, still shimmering prettily on her wrist. The star charm turned this way and that, sparkling brightly as it caught the light.

Hattie wriggled down the bed to turn off the TV and it was then that she noticed the star was now not so much sparkling as glowing. Examining it more closely, Hattie saw that the crystal charm was no longer clear but a warm yellowy-orange.

Her first thought was to take the bracelet off straight away, but the clasp was quite fiddly and Hattie couldn't open it no matter how hard she tried. Running out of ideas about how to undo the bracelet, she started to feel nervous as the charm glowed ever brighter. Then, out of the corner of her eye, she saw the old leather vet's bag on the floor. To her surprise, the lock on the bag was glowing as well!

Grabbing the bag, Hattie ran her fingers over the shimmering lock. It was in the shape of a star too!

Suddenly she knew exactly what to do.

This has got to be worth a try, Hattie thought as she carefully pressed the still-glowing star charm against the lock.

With a loud *CLICK*, the bag sprang open in Hattie's hands and a tingly feeling started to spread through her fingers.

Looking down, Hattie gasped in amazement.

The bag was turning from its dull brownish colour to a sparkly silver. The whole bag seemed to be shining. Then two letters began to appear among the silvery sparkles in a glowing purple light: *H* and *B*. The first letters of Hattie's name!

Hattie had never seen anything like it before in her whole life. What did it all mean?

With trembling hands, Hattie opened the bag and slowly peered inside. But, before she'd had a chance to have a proper look, she felt the strangest pulling feeling and heard a big *whooosh*. All of a sudden, she was tumbling down, down and down . . .

A Magical Meeting

Hattie landed with an unceremonious bump and found herself sitting on a cool, hard floor. She had no idea how far or for how long she had travelled – perhaps she'd fallen through to the other side of the world! Gingerly rubbing her sore bottom, Hattie looked around. The first thing she spotted was the silver vet's bag sparkling brightly by her pink trainers. Unsure what the bag might make her do next, Hattie didn't dare pick it up. Instead, she turned her head slowly this way and that, trying to work out where on earth she was.

Looking at the rocky walls that surrounded her, Hattie thought she might be in some sort of cave. It didn't appear to be very big, and she was surprised at how easily she could see around her as there didn't seem to be any lights or lamps. It was only when Hattie looked more closely that she realized the walls were encrusted with thousands of glittering crystals, which gave the cave a gentle and magical glow.

Then something on the closest wall caught Hattie's eye. It was a square piece of paper, attached a little crookedly with some tape. On it, in large scrawly handwriting, were just two words:

Back soon!

The note wasn't signed and the other side of the paper was blank.

Who left it here? Hattie wondered. *And when exactly will they be back?*

She decided to investigate the wall furthest from her to see if she could find any clues elsewhere. She noticed that here the rock had been hollowed out to make shelves. Each shelf was crowded with glass bottles of every possible shape and size. Some had bright liquids in them and others were wrapped in wispy

cobwebs, as if they hadn't been touched for years. Hattie couldn't imagine what they were all for.

As she ran her eyes along the very top shelf, she saw that the line of bottles was broken in the middle by a large book that was balanced precariously. The book had a red leather cover, scuffed in places, and it looked ancient. Hattie couldn't see a title, just a large and intricate faded gold design, which she thought was perhaps a dragon, though she couldn't be certain.

With no more clues as to where she was or, more importantly, how she could get home, Hattie wondered if the book might hold the answers to at least some of the questions running around her head. But she couldn't see how she would be able to reach up quite so high and pluck it from its perilous position without breaking half the higgledy-piggledy bottles on the shelf. And, without knowing exactly what was in the bottles, that was a risk Hattie definitely didn't want to take! So, instead, she decided to explore the rest of the cave.

At the heart of it was a large, round stone table. On a smaller slab of stone next to this was a shiny glass bowl containing what seemed to be tools. Hattie wandered closer to get a better look at them, and what she discovered stopped her in her tracks. They were all made of different materials – some a glowing kind of metal, others almost crystal-like – but they were exactly the same shape and size as the equipment her mum and dad used in their vet's surgery. Now Hattie was really confused! What kind of secret vet's surgery was this? It definitely wasn't part of her mum and dad's practice – that much she knew for sure. So where was she?

Hattie began to search this strange glowing cave room even further. There must be something that would help her work out what was happening. Deciding to start from the bottom, she was peering at the floor to look for clues when a loud voice boomed across the cave.

'Ah, Hattie, you're here! Welcome!'

Jumping up in surprise, Hattie only just avoided hitting her head on the hard edge of the stone table before she spotted a familiar figure entering the cave through a small wooden door at the back. Uncle B! It had been a while since Hattie had seen Mum's older brother but she recognized him immediately. He was the only other person in their family who shared her white streak of hair – and she could see it now, running through his slightly messy dark curls.

'Uncle B!' cried Hattie, delighted to see

someone she knew. 'What are *you* doing here?
Actually, I don't even know where *here* is!
Where *are* we? I've got no idea what's going on!'

'It must all seem very strange,' replied Uncle B, noticing that Hattie's look of delight was starting to change to one of anxiety. 'I've brought you a delicious cup of lilac tea. It's made from lilac petals gathered in Unicorn Meadows and it's very soothing. Here, drink it while I explain what this is all about.'

Hattie took the china cup that Uncle B held out to her, too confused to even ask where on earth Unicorn Meadows might be! The tea didn't look like anything she'd ever drunk before. It was bright purple for a start, though she had to admit the scent wafting up from it was quite soothing – and it tasted sweet and delicious.

Taking a second sip, she waited for her uncle to begin.

'There's a lot to tell,' said Uncle B, leaning wearily against the edge of the table, 'so I shall start from the very beginning. It may be a lot for you to take in, but be patient, Hattie. Everything will become clear soon. You'll have heard from your parents that I have been away travelling the world, seeing the sights and enjoying new and interesting cultures.' Hattie nodded before Uncle B carried on. 'But in fact I've never been able to tell them the complete truth as I'm bound by an ancient oath of secrecy, an oath that now binds you too. I've actually been away in the land where you find yourself now, in the magical Kingdom of Bellua, where I am Guardian to its magical creatures. I look after unicorns and fairies, mermaids and dragons – and just about any other kind of magical creature you might think of!'

'*Unicorns and fairies?*' Hattie couldn't believe what he was saying. 'Are you all right, Uncle B? Maybe you should sit down!'

Uncle B chuckled. 'I'm quite fine, Hattie – you'll soon see for yourself. I don't have much time so I must explain quickly. The Guardian's main role is to take care of these magical creatures, healing them when they're sick and making sure their magical powers are never threatened. I've carried out the role of Guardian for over thirty years now – indeed, since I was your age, Hattie. For my duties, as with all Guardians before me, I have earned the respect of every animal in this magical land. However, it's a tiring role and must be passed on to the next generation. This, Hattie, is where you come in.'

'Me?' exclaimed Hattie, feeling both shocked and a little horrified. 'How do you know?' Taking another sip of lilac tea to calm her nerves, she waited for Uncle B to explain further.

'All Guardians must be members of the Bright family,' he went on. 'But only those who share the marks of the Guardian – the white streak in their hair and the unusual star-shaped birthmark on their face – can take on this important role.'

As Uncle B moved his hair to one side to reveal a small star-shaped birthmark high on a cheekbone, Hattie raised a hand to feel the similar-shaped mark on her own right cheek.

'From a young age, Hattie, you carried both these marks and I always knew you would be my successor here in Bellua.'

Could Uncle B be right? Hattie wondered. *Am I really destined to take on this strange role?*

A hundred questions began to fill her head, but she noticed that Uncle B kept glancing towards the wooden door, as though he was anxious to get away, and so she didn't ask any of them. Instead, she listened in awe as Uncle B continued.

'I'm afraid to say that caring for the magical creatures of Bellua is just one part of the role I must pass on to you, Hattie,' he said, a look of concern crossing his face. 'There is a great threat to the peace of Bellua in the shape of Ivar, King of the Imps, who is determined to steal the magical gifts from the other creatures here. I fear his plans are grave indeed. He will stop at nothing to take what he wants, harming the creatures of Bellua wherever he goes. Your duty will always be to help any magical creature in need – but beware of those who may be working with Ivar to achieve his wicked aims.

King Ivar has no respect for the Guardian and will do everything he can to stop you succeeding in your tasks.'

A part of Hattie couldn't imagine that an Imp King could really have any power over a ten-year-old girl, but the serious look on Uncle B's face and the strange events of the day so far suggested that perhaps anything was possible after all.

'Though you must be cautious as you travel through Bellua, you will come across wonders that you couldn't even imagine, Hattie.' With a twinkle in his eye, Uncle B beckoned her towards a small window at the back of the cave. Following him, she peered outside.

'Oh . . . wow!' gasped Hattie. The colours outside were brighter than in any place she'd ever been before, and a faint shimmer and sparkle seemed to whip through the air. It was beautiful! But, before Hattie could take in any more, Uncle B strode back quickly towards the stone table.

'Bellua lies beyond that window,' he said. 'I'm sure you'll be a very successful Guardian, Hattie, and it won't be long before you have the chance to prove me right. Ah, oh yes, I almost forgot, your first patient should be here right now,' said Uncle B, glancing around. 'Her name is Mith Ickle and I'm afraid she has already encountered King Ivar. The evil imp threw some dust in poor Mith Ickle's face and, once she had finished coughing and spluttering, she discovered that Ivar had stolen her flame, and with it her beautiful voice.'

'Oh my goodness!' said Hattie as she looked around the cave, wondering where on earth the creature could be.

'My goodness indeed!' chortled Uncle B. 'I know you'll be able to return it to her, Hattie – the fate of Bellua really does rest in your hands now!'

'But, Uncle B, how will I –?' Hattie hadn't even finished her question before Uncle B had grabbed the sparkly vet's bag from where she'd left it on the floor.

'I must go, Hattie,' he said. 'There can only

be one Guardian in Bellua and already I can feel myself being pushed away. You don't mind if I borrow this, do you? And don't forget – you mustn't tell anyone about Bellua, not even your parents or very best friend. Remember, you are bound to an ancient oath of secrecy! Don't worry – you'll be brilliant! Cheerio!'

Hattie watched with astonishment as her uncle peered into the bag and instantly disappeared. The bag snapped shut and looked like an ordinary vet's bag again, though still a bit sparkly.

Before she had a chance to puzzle over what had just happened, Hattie was interrupted by a tiny muffled sneeze. She jumped in shock. The sneeze seemed to have come from under the stone table, so, inching over as quietly as she could, Hattie dipped her head to peer beneath it.

For a moment Hattie felt like she could hardly breathe.

There, under the table, sat a tiny pink dragon.

Inside the Big Book

Face to face with the tiny creature, Hattie stared in wonder. The dragon's long tail was curled round her body and she gazed back at Hattie with large, dark, dreamy eyes, framed by the longest eyelashes she had ever seen.

Mith Ickle opened her mouth and made the quietest of croaks, accompanied by a little puff of grey smoke. Hattie sat back in surprise. Was the poor thing trying to speak to her? Although she couldn't be sure, Hattie guessed that the dragon was really too small to be much of a danger. She crept a little closer to her smoking snout and, on Mith Ickle's next attempt, Hattie could just make out the words: 'No fire, no voice!'

Remembering what Uncle B had told her, Hattie knew she had to help, but she didn't know where to begin. This was a *dragon*, after all! Not one of the puppies, kittens or rabbits that Hattie saw regularly at her mum and dad's vet's practice. Hattie was trying to imagine how her parents might cope with the unlikely problem of a dragon in distress in their own surgery when, suddenly, Mith Ickle spread her pink wings and fluttered past Hattie's face.

Hattie flinched, scared that the little dragon might be more dangerous than she had first thought. However, Mith Ickle carried on flying, towards the big red book that Hattie had seen on the cave shelf. On reaching it, she flapped her wings faster, hovering and scratching at the battered cover with her clawed feet. She nodded her snout towards Hattie, who thought she must be trying to tell her something about the book, before flying back down and perching on the large stone table.

'Do you want me to look at the book?' Hattie asked, before adding, 'It's just that I don't think I can get it down without knocking things everywhere.' She hoped that the dragon could actually understand her.

It soon became obvious that Mith Ickle had understood everything. She flew back to the top shelf and began delicately picking up the fragile glass bottles in her claws one at a time. Gently, she placed each bottle on a different shelf, until none were left near enough to the book for Hattie to knock over. Then she scratched again at the book's cover and looked hopefully in Hattie's direction.

Hattie climbed up on to the table to get

as close to the book as she could. Now that the bottles had been moved, Hattie could lean her weight on the shelf and take a better look. She noticed that, like the sparkly vet's bag, the book had a gold star-shaped lock on one side.

Could the star charm work twice in one day? Hattie wondered.

She reached up and very carefully lifted the book off the shelf. It was even heavier than it looked and Hattie only just managed to place it on the table without dropping it. She jumped off the table and, holding her breath with anticipation, she slowly pressed her star charm into the book's lock. The charm and lock glowed brightly against the dim light of the cave. Then the lock gave a satisfying *click* as it opened.

Smiling in relief, Hattie turned to the first page but it appeared to be completely blank. Hattie was puzzled, and it was only the excited puffing of the little dragon beside her that kept her looking down as words slowly began to appear across the thick cream paper as if by magic:

Healing Magickal Beastes & Creatures

Hattie guessed this must be the title of the book and, with shaking hands, she started to flick through the well-thumbed pages. There were no clear chapters, and every page seemed to be made up of a crowded mixture of drawings, diagrams, lists and instructions. And none of them seemed to be about animals that Hattie recognized. In fact, she could have sworn that she saw pictures of unicorns and fairies – and even yetis at one point. She could hardly believe what she was seeing, but, then again, there *was* a tiny dragon beside her!

Hattie felt the warm puff of Mith Ickle's breath as she peered over her shoulder. She wondered if Mith Ickle might be able to help her find her way around the book, but the creature looked as confused as Hattie felt.

Eventually, Hattie came across a page entitled 'Dragons & Dragon-Like Beastes'. At first she could only see lists of what she guessed must be different types of dragon. But further on she spotted a picture of a dragon that looked very similar to the little pink one now hovering excitedly over the open book. Hattie watched in amazement as words began to appear beside the drawing as if by magic.

This little dragon, with its fire lost, has no voice and is in mortal danger. No more may it sing those ancient lullabies that cause its enemies to fall into a deepe sleepe. And thus awake, these same enemies will ever more hunte and steale this dragon's precious scales.

The strange English was a little hard to understand and Hattie found herself talking aloud as she tried to make sense of it.

'Oh, that's why King Ivar has stolen your voice, Mith!' she began, before adding, 'You don't mind me calling you Mith, do you? It's just that Mith Ickle's quite a long name. I'm called Harriet really, but everyone calls me Hattie – it's so much easier.' Seeing Mith Ickle nod with a little smile, Hattie continued with her musings. 'So if King Ivar has your voice he can use it to send his enemies to sleep, just like you do. But without your voice you can't defend yourself, you poor thing.'

Since dragon enemies hunted them for their scales, Hattie realized that, without her voice, Mith Ickle was indeed in quite a lot of danger!

Hattie only had to glance at the dragon, now nodding sadly by her side, to realize that Mith Ickle understood this danger completely. Her unhappy little face reminded Hattie of the many frightened animals that she had cared for at her parents' surgery. Hattie decided she had to do whatever she could to help Mith Ickle get better.

'Don't worry, Mith – we'll have you singing again in no time.' Hattie's soothing voice had always calmed the animals in her parents' surgery, and she was relieved to see that it had the same effect in Bellua. Seeing Mith Ickle relax slightly, she smiled to herself with a new confidence.

Maybe I'll be a brilliant Guardian after all, she thought. *Just like Uncle B said.*

That is, until she remembered what he'd also told her about King Ivar . . .

Into the
Magical Kingdom

Hattie flicked through the next few pages of the book, but they didn't look like they were going to help much. The drawings were of different dragons and the ailments were things like burns to the mouth, missing tail tips and cracked claws. There was nothing about a dragon losing its fire or voice.

She was about to close the book in frustration

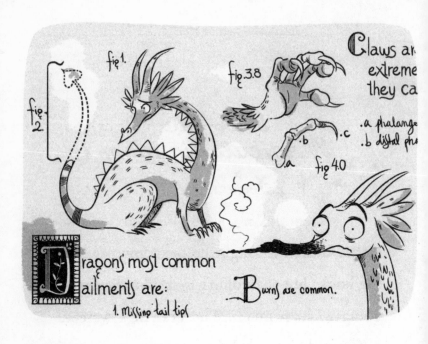

when the small pink dragon began flapping her wings wildly.

'Don't worry, Mith. I know you need help to get better and I'm going to try my very hardest, I promise. Uncle B thinks I can do it and I really don't want to let him down,' she said.

Hattie's soft voice soothed the little dragon, and she nuzzled her new Guardian's cheek to show that she understood her.

'Let's keep looking, Mith,' said Hattie. 'The answer *must* be somewhere in this book.'

Mith Ickle nodded earnestly. After skimming through several more pages of intricate drawings, Hattie eventually found a picture of a dragon that looked just like Mith Ickle: small and softly coloured with a blush of pink. A large cross was drawn across its snout to indicate its missing voice and fire. Underneath the drawing, a smaller illustration showed a red flower next to a bottle of clear liquid and, next to that, a red drink being dripped into the pink dragon's mouth. Beside the picture, Hattie read the words:

Sunray Flower + Boiled Enchanted Water = Dragon Drink as Hot as the Hottest Chilli to Refreshe Fire & Voice

It seemed to be some sort of prescription, though Hattie had no idea how to make the suggested medicine. Looking along the rows of what she now guessed to be potion bottles, she spotted one labelled ENCHANTED WATER and carefully lifted it down to the table. But there were none labelled SUNRAY FLOWER, and it was only when Mith Ickle began scratching at the book that Hattie looked at the open page again.

There at the bottom she found a riddle

written in scratchy black ink that was incredibly difficult to read. Hattie read aloud, stumbling over the words, and hoping that it might start to mean something to either her or Mith Ickle.

Source the flower from the rumbling heat,
Let not the fire's depth see you beat.
Pluck it sure, without pause to think,
Then the dragon does well to drink.

Hattie scratched her head, thinking hard. Was the riddle telling her where she could find the sunray flower? Before she had time to try to make sense of it, she gasped in amazement as a piece of paper fluttered out of the pages of the book and flattened itself on the table in front of her.

Hattie looked at Mith Ickle, and the little pink dragon nodded at her encouragingly. Taking comfort from her new friend's presence, Hattie ran her finger along the old but blank piece of paper, wondering what it could mean.

She felt a tingle under her fingertip as a detailed and beautiful map suddenly blossomed on to the paper. Different areas appeared, marked with pictures of trees, rivers, mountains and seas that had names Hattie had only ever imagined existed in storybooks: UNICORN MEADOWS, FAIRY FOREST, RAINBOW WATERFALL... Hattie couldn't believe that these were real places – but, even if they were, it didn't tell her which of them might be home to the sunray flower.

'How on earth is this map going to help me to help you?' an exasperated Hattie asked Mith Ickle. 'Especially when I don't even know where *I* am!'

Mith Ickle gently fluttered from the table to Hattie's shoulder and pointed to the wooden door at the back of the cave, the one that Uncle B had come through earlier. Clutching the map, Hattie headed towards it, with Mith Ickle fluttering alongside. With just a moment's hesitation as she summoned up her courage, Hattie pushed open the door and walked outside.

Now able to take in more than a glimpse of Bellua, Hattie couldn't believe what she was seeing. Her eyes widened in wonder at the scene in front of her. Across a backdrop of lush green fields and hills covered in every colour of flower, magical creatures of all shapes and sizes stood, fluttered and galloped.

If Hattie hadn't already met Mith Ickle, she would have thought she was dreaming as magnificent unicorns galloped by, delicate and beautiful fairies peered from trees and flowers, and even pixies scampered past. Here, it was as though all the world's fairy stories were *actually real*!

'The magical Kingdom of Bellua,' Hattie

whispered to herself. *I can't believe that anyone would want to harm this place. I won't let that happen!*

She knew then that she would take on *all* the duties required of a Guardian — and the sound of Mith Ickle's lightly beating wings reminded her that she needed to start with her first patient.

Hattie looked around and noticed a beautiful shimmering stream in the distance and a tall snow-covered mountain range behind her. The dragon swept down towards the map, and Hattie pointed to an area labelled VALLEY OF THE GUARDIANS.

'Is this where we are now?' she asked.

Mith Ickle nodded and Hattie felt pleased that she was finally getting somewhere. Looking at the map again, Hattie read out the names of the places on it — SILVERY STREAM, ENCHANTED ORCHARD, RUMBLING VOLCANO . . .

'Rumbling Volcano!' Hattie shouted the name out so loudly that Mith Ickle jumped in the air. 'That's what it said in the riddle,' Hattie explained excitedly. 'It talked about finding a flower in the rumbling heat. That's where I have to go to find the sunray flower that will give you back your voice!'

Hattie was just about to start walking when she felt Mith Ickle's warm body curl round her neck, her tail coming to rest on Hattie's left shoulder.

'Come too,' croaked Mith Ickle, sending a puff of smoke up Hattie's nose, which made her sneeze loudly.

Hattie wondered whether a poorly dragon should really be heading off on what might be a dangerous expedition, but she'd already grown fond of her little pink friend – and, besides, Mith Ickle knew far more about the Kingdom of Bellua than Hattie did, which was reassuring because she knew next to nothing. Hattie also hoped that Mith Ickle might be able to help her get home again – once she had got the poor dragon's voice back, of course.

For now, though, Hattie was keen to do Uncle B proud and prove that she could be a worthy Guardian. Taking her first steps into Bellua, Hattie couldn't help feeling a little nervous and knew she would be grateful to have a friendly companion by her side.

'Come on then, Mith,' said Hattie. 'Let's go!'

Testing Trolls

Checking the map at every turn, Hattie and Mith Ickle began to make their way across the magical Kingdom of Bellua.

Hattie felt like she had stepped into the pages of a fairy tale as they passed through a wide silver arch decorated with glowing ancient symbols. According to the map, they had now entered Unicorn Meadows.

All around Hattie, unicorns gently galloped past over the lush green fields that were dotted with every kind of flower she could imagine. Some of the smaller unicorns were almost hidden by tall grasses, with only their horn poking up now and again to show that they were there. The unicorns had manes of many colours, with some of the most beautiful having all the colours of the rainbow flowing together in their long swishing tails.

Hattie was just about to pinch herself to make sure she wasn't dreaming when she felt something gently nuzzle her neck. Expecting it to be Mith Ickle, she turned round and jumped in surprise when she saw a tall white unicorn with a long lilac mane standing right behind her.

'I see you have the mark of a Guardian,' said the unicorn in a rich, melodic voice, bobbing his head towards the birthmark on Hattie's cheek. 'As I have welcomed your uncle before you, so I welcome you to Unicorn Meadows. I am Themis, leader of the unicorns of Bellua. Your task ahead is great, Guardian. King Ivar will stop at nothing to gain more power and many creatures will be in danger. We wish you well and, should you need our help, we will always be here.'

Standing there in awe, Hattie struggled to say anything back without stuttering or saying something silly. Themis was so beautiful that

Hattie's tongue seemed to be tied. But it turned out that the unicorn leader was anxious to tell her something else.

'I know not where you are heading, but let me offer this advice,' continued Themis. 'The fairies of Bellua are full of magical mischief. Be sure only to pass by the Fairy Forest – *do not enter it*. Only then can you be certain of a safe and speedy passage through our kingdom.'

Before Hattie could open her mouth to say thank you, Themis dipped his head in a majestic bow to both her and Mith Ickle, then turned on his hooves and galloped back into the meadow to join the unicorn herd.

'Well, Mith, I think our journey has just got

a lot longer, and it could be more complicated than I thought,' Hattie said, opening the map out as much as she could. The little dragon curled protectively round her shoulders.

Hattie could see the Rumbling Volcano – and the Fairy Forest which stood between it and where she was now. The only other way of getting to the volcano was to cross the stream at a place marked TROLL BRIDGE, which Hattie didn't fancy at all! The Fairy Forest definitely sounded like it *ought* to be the better route, but, after Themis's warning, Hattie wasn't sure that there were any safe options in Bellua at all.

For the first time, Hattie began to wonder if

she was in real danger. She didn't want to admit it to Mith Ickle, but she was actually feeling quite scared. She was even starting to question whether she was the right person to be the new Guardian of Bellua after all.

Uncle B seemed so sure that I should take over from him, thought Hattie. *I won't let him down.*

Taking a deep breath, she looked once more at the map. Mith Ickle was relying on her – and so were Uncle B and all of Bellua. Hattie *had* to be brave.

'OK, Mith,' she said. 'Neither of us wants to meet trolls but we don't have any other choice.' Mith Ickle nuzzled Hattie's cheek to show that she agreed with her new Guardian. Hattie smiled and, looking at her friend, she said, 'As long as we're together, I'm sure we'll be fine.'

With that, she folded the map and started walking, leaving Unicorn Meadows behind them.

The route took Hattie and Mith Ickle round the edge of the Fairy Forest, which was bordered by tall bushy trees with leaves in every shade of red, orange, yellow and green. Among the branches, Hattie could see many sparkling fairies glittering and twinkling as they flitted about.

The fairies saw the pair walking past and called to them in soft, high-pitched voices: 'Come here, come and play with us!' and 'Please come in and be our friend!'

Hattie couldn't believe such pretty little

creatures were capable of causing so much trouble and she was tempted to go with them as they gently tugged at her clothes and hair, in the direction of the Fairy Forest. However,

looking at Mith Ickle's wary expression and remembering the unicorn's warning, she smiled back at them but walked firmly on.

Hattie was just starting to wonder when they would reach the end of the forest when, at last, she glimpsed the foot of the Rumbling Volcano. Hattie could see the steaming mountain rising up in front of them, but the path to it was blocked by a bridge that was guarded by a solid line of six very unfriendly looking trolls. She felt Mith Ickle settle nervously on her shoulder as she walked towards them, her chest thumping with fear at their glaring eyes.

'STOP!' bellowed the shortest of the trolls before Hattie had taken more than a few steps. 'Only a true Guardian can cross this bridge and approach the Rumbling Volcano. And her friend, I suppose,' he added, pointing a chubby, long-nailed finger in the direction of Mith Ickle.

'Answer this riddle and prove your worth,' said another of the trolls, this one a large, chunky creature. He removed a scroll from his pocket and, with grubby fingers ending in bitten nails, slowly unrolled it and read aloud.

'To show you are a Guardian true,
Reveal a jewel from the sky so blue.'

Hattie was puzzled. What kind of jewel could the troll mean? There was nothing in the sky, even in this world, that Hattie would consider

a jewel. She didn't think they meant the sun –
or the moon if it were night. And how would
she *reveal* those anyway?

Hattie was ready to give up and simply beg
the trolls to let them pass, or even to make a
run for the volcano past the trolls, but then
Mith Ickle fluttered down and pointed to the
bracelet on Hattie's wrist. The star charm was
glowing brightly.

Of course, thought Hattie. *The star!*

She held her wrist up, but all the trolls shook
their heads. Hattie's heart sank. How would
they ever get through?

The troll with the riddle began reading from
his scroll again.

'Show not false stars nor be untrue,
This star must be thine and only of you!'

Hattie was a little hurt. She didn't think she'd been untrue, but she knew she needed to show them another star — and fast!

Then, suddenly, it dawned on Hattie — she *did* know what they wanted after all and wondered how she could have been so forgetful! Mith Ickle looked at her curiously as Hattie turned the right side of her face towards the trolls, rubbing hard at the star-shaped birthmark on her cheek to show them that it couldn't be removed.

Satisfied at last, the oldest of the trolls,

who was almost bent double with age, walked towards Hattie.

'You may pass, Guardian,' he declared, before looking at Mith Ickle and sneering, 'and you, Guardian's *pet*.'

Mith Ickle blushed, her pink cheeks turning bright red as the troll's mean comment hit home.

'She is *not* my pet,' Hattie declared indignantly on behalf of the little dragon. 'She is my good friend.'

The old troll shrugged, but said nothing.

The line of trolls split in two and Hattie strode across the bridge. Still angry on Mith Ickle's behalf, she stopped halfway across and turned round to tell the troll what she really thought of him, but the dragon tugged at her sleeve with her claws and pulled her back.

'Not worth it,' she croaked with a puff of smoke. 'Must get sunray flower.'

Hattie gazed into Mith Ickle's dark eyes. 'Only if you're sure, Mith. I'm the Guardian and I will look after you.'

Mith Ickle nodded with determination.

'Come on then,' said Hattie. 'Let's get you that sunray flower!'

Hattie stroked the dragon's smooth scales as they made their way to the base of the Rumbling Volcano. She looked back only once, noticing that the trolls had joined

together once again: a firm barrier between the volcano and the rest of the Kingdom of Bellua.

With no hope of going back, even if she had

wanted to, Hattie looked up at the huge mountain ahead of her. She could already feel its heat pricking at her skin as she took her first step on to its red-hot, ash-covered sides.

A Scramble
and a Scrape

At first, Hattie's pink trainers just sank into the soft ash and she couldn't imagine how she would ever climb all the way to the top of the huge volcano. It was Mith Ickle who set her on the right path, staying by Hattie's shoulder and swooping down every now and then to point out a branch or rock that Hattie could grab on to or use as a foothold. The ash made her eyes watery and her throat dry, and both Hattie and Mith Ickle sneezed many times as it crept into their noses.

The climb was tiring work and Hattie thought it was a bit like a game of snakes and ladders. She would go up a bit, then slip and slide back to where she had started so that she had to begin that part of the climb all over again. But it wasn't just the odd chunk of loose rock that bothered Hattie. Every time a stone tumbled, she thought she saw a flash of blue so bright it couldn't possibly be volcano ash. With Uncle B's warning still fresh in her mind, Hattie couldn't help worrying that King Ivar was already trying to stop her in her tracks. Doing her best to ignore the ball of nerves forming in her tummy, she wondered if she was just being paranoid – and whether the bright colours of Bellua had simply gone to her head.

When they were about halfway up the volcano, Hattie's legs were feeling tired and shaky. Spotting a rocky ledge just a few steps away, she wondered if there was time for a short rest.

'I expect your wings need a break too,' said Hattie, patting the rock in an invitation for Mith Ickle, who was hovering protectively beside her, to settle there for a minute or two. The little dragon accepted the offer gratefully, folding away her tired wings as Hattie perched on the ledge and took in the view.

'Wow! This is amazing!' Hattie exclaimed, realizing just how high up they now were. She could see right across the magical Kingdom of Bellua. There were fields of many colours, trees of all heights and even different-coloured sections of sky. To her left, a dark sky seemed to twinkle with a million tiny stars. To her right, a pale blue sky was criss-crossed by at least a hundred rainbows. Hattie could never have imagined anywhere like it!

I wonder if Uncle B has ever climbed up this high? she thought. Hattie tried to imagine him scrabbling through the ash and rocks to where

she now sat. She hoped that she'd see him again soon, because she knew he was the only person she could talk to about her adventure. Thinking of Uncle B reminded Hattie of the important role he'd passed on to her and she jumped up again, eager to continue with her first task as Guardian.

'Come on, Mith,' she said, beckoning the dragon to follow her as she began scrambling up the side of the volcano again. 'Let's keep going and look for that flower, shall we? Then I can help you get back your beautiful voice.'

Mith Ickle didn't need much encouragement and Hattie was grateful to have her friend flying beside her again. Not only did Hattie enjoy the company but the gentle flapping of Mith Ickle's wings acted like a fan, cooling Hattie down as the Rumbling Volcano became hotter and hotter the higher she climbed. It also, Hattie noticed, lived up to its name – beneath her hands and feet she could feel the mountain rumbling and grumbling as if it might erupt at any moment. Hattie tried to put that thought out of her mind and carried on.

The more the volcano rumbled, the more rubble and rocks it sent tumbling down its steaming sides. Small stones brushed Hattie's ankles, and once or twice she had to jump over larger rocks that threatened to knock her right off her feet. Mith Ickle could fly above these mini landslides, but it was while the little dragon was crouching down in the middle of yet another sneeze that Hattie spotted a large boulder rolling down the volcano – heading straight for her new friend.

'Mith' she called. 'Quick! Move!'

But Mith Ickle had her wings folded across her snout and didn't hear her.

'Please, Mith!' Hattie cried, watching the boulder pick up speed. 'The rock!'

It was no use.

Without stopping to think, Hattie threw herself across the rock's path and pushed Mith Ickle away from it with all her strength.

'Ow!' Hattie cried as the boulder scraped past her hand, badly grazing her skin.

The heat of the volcano made the injury sting even more and Hattie felt tears spring up in her eyes at the pain.

Mith Ickle immediately flew to Hattie's side. 'Saved me,' croaked the pink dragon with a gentle puff of smoke. 'Save you too.'

Before Hattie had time to ask what she meant, Mith Ickle had stuck out her little blue forked tongue and bent her scaly head down towards Hattie's injured hand.

Hattie felt herself flinch, expecting the dragon's tongue to scratch her already sore hand, but Mith Ickle's pointy tongue didn't hurt her at all – it just tingled as the dragon began to gently lick her wound. To Hattie's surprise, the pain stopped almost immediately. After less than a minute, Hattie was even more amazed to see the graze start to heal up and disappear.

'That's incredible! Thank you. Thank you so much,' she said, gazing at her restored hand as Mith Ickle hovered again by her shoulder.

'Friend,' puffed the little dragon.

Hattie smiled as the warm glow of friendship enveloped her. 'Friend,' she agreed, stroking the top of Mith Ickle's head fondly. 'Now let's find you that sunray flower!'

As they got used to the sweltering heat, the rumbling ground beneath their feet and the tumbling rubble, Hattie and Mith Ickle found they could climb faster. Before they knew it, they came to a large, flat ledge just a few metres below the summit of the Rumbling Volcano. Hattie couldn't help whooping with joy when she saw that it was covered with huge clumps of bright red flowers. Even Mith Ickle managed to puff out her own croaky cheer.

'These must be the sunray flowers we need, Mith!' shouted Hattie, bending down to pick a bunch.

But, when she looked more closely, Hattie realized that not all the red flowers were the same. Some had long thin petals, while others had shorter round ones. Some had a soft yellow middle and others had a hard black one. Now she wasn't sure which to pick after all.

'How do we know which flowers will give

you back your fire?' she asked Mith Ickle.
Although she was completely exhausted after
her climb, Hattie knew she couldn't give
up now; she had to help her friend get better.

She looked at Mith Ickle's hopeful face and remembered that the poorly dragon was completely relying on her. Hattie sat down and put her head in her hands, desperately trying to recall exactly what the book had said.

'That's it!' Hattie jumped up. 'We need to find the flower that's as hot as a chilli. Help me try them, Mith!'

Hattie watched as the little dragon began swooping in and out of the clumps of flowers, taking small bites from the petals of each different one she passed. It was only when Hattie saw her stick out her blue tongue with a croaky 'Ouch!' that she knew Mith Ickle had found the right flower.

Just then, the volcano rumbled so loudly that Hattie almost fell over with shock. She scrambled over to Mith Ickle and the sunray flower, and bent down to pick as many as she could – the volcano trembling ominously beneath her trainers. With her friend's help, Hattie was soon clutching a huge bunch of the bright red flowers.

'Come on, let's get out of here!' she called as the volcano roared louder than ever.

The journey back down the mountain was shorter and less tiring. With Mith Ickle by her side, Hattie scrambled and slid back down as fast as her legs (or more often her bottom) could carry her, holding the bunch of flowers tightly to her body to avoid dropping them.

Then, at last, she was back at the foot of the volcano, a little bruised and dusty – and once more face to face with the line of unfriendly looking trolls.

All Alone Again

This time the trolls had no riddles for Hattie. They simply parted with solemn looks on their faces, gesturing to Mith Ickle and Hattie to pass. Hattie turned round and stuck her tongue out at the back of the eldest troll, the one who had been so mean to Mith Ickle. She drew in her breath sharply as she realized that one of the other trolls, the smallest and youngest of them all, had spotted her. Should she run? But then the troll gave her a cheeky grin and stuck its tongue back out at her.

Hattie laughed and caught Mith Ickle's twinkling eye. Perhaps the trolls weren't so bad after all.

Hattie had just pulled out the map to work out the best way back to the cave (avoiding the Fairy Forest, of course) when a delicate little creature with pointy features and blue hair in pretty bunches danced towards her.

'Immie the Imp, pleased to meet you,' sang the creature in a flute-like voice, arriving at Hattie's feet. 'You must be Hattie.'

How does she know who I am? wondered

Hattie. At first glance, she thought that Immie looked more than a little like Victoria Frost, who had been so nasty to her earlier that morning.

'I've met your Uncle B lots of times. He's so helpful to us creatures, and I see he's teaching you to be helpful too,' continued Immie. 'Aren't those sunray flowers you've collected? You must need to get those home. Would you like me to tell you about a shortcut?'

Hattie nodded, realizing how silly she'd been to compare this nice girl to someone as mean as Victoria.

As soon as Immie had shown her the route, Hattie thanked her and set off. With Mith Ickle helping her to follow the map, Hattie soon found her way down Elf Avenue and took the secret route through Pixie Park that Immie had pointed out to her. It was at the other end of the park, with the Winter Mountains looming ahead of them, that Hattie first began to shiver. Thinking it must just be the heat of the Rumbling Volcano starting to leave her body, she sped up a little to keep warm.

'Come on, Mith!' she called. 'Immie said to take the first path we see through the mountains. This looks like it – we'll be almost home once we've got to the end!'

However, as they travelled further along the path, it became so cold that Hattie's teeth began to chatter. She could even see her breath in front of her. Hattie turned towards Mith Ickle, who didn't seem to feel the cold but had a worried look on her face and was shaking her head from side to side.

'What is it?' asked Hattie, starting to feel a little anxious. 'We took the right path, didn't we?' Mith Ickle nodded. 'And Immie did tell us the right way to go, didn't she?'

This time Mith Ickle didn't nod but shook her head sadly.

'You don't think she tricked us, do you?' asked Hattie unhappily, realizing that she had had no real reason to trust the imp just because she was friendly and knew her name.

'What are we going to do?' Hattie asked, her teeth chattering furiously now.

Mith Ickle gazed at Hattie, a serious expression

on her face. She puffed out some grey misty smoke that warmed Hattie a little. Then she rose up in the air, croaking just two words: 'Fly now.'

Hattie watched in horror as Mith Ickle started flapping her wings before heading back the way they had come!

'Mith!' cried Hattie desperately. 'Where are you going?'

Hattie began to panic. Surely Mith Ickle wasn't going to leave her alone in the frozen mountains? 'No!' she cried. 'Don't leave me! You can't!'

Mith Ickle paused, hovering for just a moment. She turned back to Hattie. 'Trust me,' she croaked, and then she flew away.

Hattie couldn't believe this was happening again. Not only had her mum, dad and very best friend let her down that morning but now even Mith Ickle had left her when she needed her most. Hattie curled up on the frozen path and began to sob.

With each sniff, her eyelids became more droopy and her arms and legs felt heavier and heavier. Just as Hattie began to drop off to sleep, a deep cackling laugh echoed around the Winter Mountains . . .

Hattie had no idea how long she'd been asleep when she woke up – and she didn't have a clue where she was! Hattie was sure she had fallen asleep in the snow, but now, enveloped by darkness, she felt as toasty as could be. As she came to her senses, Hattie shivered as she thought about the scary laughter she'd heard earlier and hoped it wasn't King Ivar. Surely it had been a bad dream!

She sat up and the darkness fell away. Gradually she could see that she'd been surrounded by a wall of dragons, who had breathed warm air on her. Hattie realized she had also been covered in the warmest and softest of furs.

Hattie's eyes were widening in fear when Mith Ickle came fluttering over the dragons to land on her shoulder.

'Friends,' Mith Ickle croaked, nodding at the circle of dragons of all different colours and sizes.

'You came back for me,' Hattie whispered gratefully.

A large, bright red dragon stepped forward. 'Hattie, if Mith Ickle still had her voice, it would be she who would speak about the things I am about to tell you, not I.'

Hattie had no idea what the dragon meant, but she could see Mith Ickle nodding at her larger friend. The other dragons continued to puff warm but thankfully fireless air down on to Hattie, thawing the last of the tears that had frozen on her face.

'There have been rumours of an imp who is working for the wicked King Ivar,' began Mith Ickle's friend. 'Some of the creatures of Bellua have said this imp plans to do anything she can to stop the Guardian from carrying out her job.

We now believe you encountered that imp at the bottom of the Rumbling Volcano. Her name is Immie. She deliberately pointed you to the wrong path, hoping that you would freeze so that she would then be able to steal the sunray flowers from your frostbitten hands.

'Mith Ickle realized that is exactly what would have happened if you'd stayed in the Winter Mountains too long. Your uncle had never crossed these icy mountains without the magical furs that cover you now – furs that Mith knew were still hanging on their special hook back in the cave. More importantly than this, with her fire still missing, Mith had no way of keeping you warm enough to complete your journey. So your new friend made the difficult decision to fly away to come to find us. She asked us to stay with you and to keep you warm while she fetched the magical furs, and so saved your life. It is an honour to be able to help you, Guardian, as we know you will help us.'

Hattie looked up at the red dragon gratefully before turning to her little pink friend. 'Oh, Mith, I'm so sorry I didn't believe in your friendship as much as I should have. I was far too quick to judge you – and thank you, dragons, for saving my life.'

Mith Ickle nuzzled Hattie's neck, playfully

blowing small puffs of smoke to tickle her nose, and Hattie knew she had been forgiven.

'You can always trust those in your life who love you, Hattie,' the big red dragon advised gently, before rising up in the air and leading the other dragons away with him.

'Farewell, Hattie B!' they called.

Hattie blushed, thinking of how grumpy she had been with her parents and what she had written in her hasty letter to Chloe. Should she have waited a little bit longer and trusted them?

Hattie shook away these thoughts, realizing there was nothing she could do about that now.

What she needed to think about was getting back to the cave as soon as possible!

'Will you be able to lead us out of these mountains, Mith?' she asked.

Mith Ickle nodded and flew up in the air. Pulling a magical fur tightly round her, Hattie followed her friend through the winding maze of mountain-range paths.

They were only a few steps beyond the mountains when Hattie and Mith Ickle spotted Immie, stamping her feet crossly and muttering something about never getting her hands on those sunray flowers to stop the Guardian now.

'Hey, Immie!' shouted Hattie, feeling anger rising inside her. 'You tried to trick us! That was really mean.'

Immie didn't answer at first but instead pointed her little snub nose up at the sky before calling back, 'Really, Hattie, isn't it a bit strange to have a *dragon* as a friend?' Then she sneered nastily, 'I mean, you don't even really live here, do you?'

Hattie felt her cheeks begin to flush, as they had when Victoria taunted her across her front garden earlier that morning. Then she felt Mith Ickle curl herself round her shoulders, and the warm act of friendship reminded Hattie that she didn't have to listen to Immie's insults.

'Well, it's better than having no friends at all, isn't it, Immie?' she replied, but Immie didn't answer. Instead, she turned on her heels and stomped off sulkily into a large clump of berry-laden bushes.

'Come on, Mith,' said Hattie, grinning at

her dragon friend and feeling proud of herself for finding the strength to stand up to Immie.

Hattie thought Mith Ickle looked like she was proud of her too. The little dragon breathed out an admiring puff of smoke and began to lead the way to the cave again.

Fire and Song

Hattie felt quite different on the journey back: more confident and a lot happier. Even the fairies in the Fairy Forest seemed to sense her change of mood and didn't try to entice her to join their mischievous games as she passed.

Hattie gave a sigh of relief when they reached the wooden door of the cave in the Valley of the Guardians. Once inside, she went straight to the stone table and laid down the bunch of sunray flowers. The large red book was still there, open at the page Hattie had been reading before she had set off, and the sparkly vet's bag was beside it.

'Sunray flower plus boiled enchanted water,' she read aloud, reminding herself of the prescription for giving a dragon back its fire, while Mith Ickle flapped around excitedly. Hattie reached for the bottle of enchanted water, glad she'd found it earlier. Now all she had to do was boil it.

After searching the cave high and low, Hattie spotted a cupboard cut into the cave wall. She had to pull hard to open its carved wooden door

but inside she was pleased to find something
that looked like a sort of stove, a small beaker
and a candle, all piled together in one corner
next to an almost empty box of matches.

Back at the table, Hattie turned to Mith Ickle, who was now swooping and diving around the cave with excitement at the prospect of getting her fire back.

'Right,' said Hattie, 'I think that's everything I need. Now, I just need to work out how to boil that enchanted water.' Using a rock as a seat at the table, she began to flick through the pages of the big red book until she found a page entitled 'Equipmente for Magickal Spelle-Making'. At the bottom of the page was a diagram that showed how to set up the old-fashioned stove and light it.

Following the picture closely, Hattie soon had the water boiling. She tore off a handful of sunray petals, feeling a slight burning tingle against her skin, and dropped them into the water, instantly turning it bright red.

While she left the potion to cool, she tore off the rest of the sunray petals and put them in an empty bottle she'd found in a corner of the cave. When Hattie added her bottle of petals to the crowded shelves, she couldn't help wondering which Guardians of Bellua had put all the other bottles there. With a flush of pride, Hattie *hoped* she might be a worthy successor to Uncle B after all.

But, to really *believe* it, Hattie knew she had to treat her first magical creature – and Mith Ickle was waiting eagerly on the stone table. Hattie found a small dropper in the bowl of vet's instruments and lowered it into the pan of warm red liquid.

'Right, Mith, are you ready?' she asked a little nervously, holding the filled dropper by the pink dragon's mouth. Mith Ickle nodded impatiently. 'OK, open up. Let's see if I can give you back your fire . . .'

Just as Hattie was about to drop the liquid into Mith Ickle's mouth, they heard little footsteps padding around outside. Turning away from her patient, Hattie glimpsed a flash of blue streaking past the window at the back of the cave. It only took a moment for Hattie to remember where she'd seen something that colour blue before –

Immie's hair! Realizing that the cave door was still open, Hattie leapt up and bolted it shut, barely a second before Immie could dart into the cave.

'I'll stop you next time, Hattie B!' called the imp, her voice muffled by the closed door but still loud enough for Hattie and Mith Ickle to hear. 'You won't get past me again, not on King Ivar's crown!'

Hattie shrugged her shoulders. 'We'll see about that, shall we, Immie?' she retorted, before turning back to her patiently waiting dragon friend.

'At last, Mith! This should bring back your voice,' said Hattie, picking up the dropper.

Mith Ickle opened her mouth as wide as she could, showing Hattie her forked, blue healing tongue and a line of sharp little teeth that ran round the top and bottom of her jaw. Hattie

remembered how gently Mith Ickle had cared for her hand when it had been grazed by the rock and so, just as carefully, Hattie released a few drops of the sunray-flower potion into Mith Ickle's mouth.

The effect of the liquid, however, was anything but gentle. First, Mith Ickle's cheeks took on a reddish glow. Then she began to cough and splutter, releasing increasingly large puffs of smoke from her nostrils. Finally, she gave a small hiccup, followed by several larger ones, and then – all of a sudden – a huge flame shot from Mith Ickle's snout halfway across the cave!

Quickly jumping out of the way, Hattie

gave a shout of joy. 'We did it! You've got your fire back!'

'It was you who did it, Hattie. Thank you,' replied Mith Ickle – and for the first time Hattie heard her voice not as a croak but sounding as sweet and beautiful as a hundred-strong choir. 'You gave me back my fire and my voice. You will have the support of us dragons for evermore. Without you, King Ivar would bring sorrow to the whole of Bellua. The peace of our beautiful magical kingdom lies in your hands.' Hattie didn't have time to think about this daunting prospect before Mith Ickle spoke again: 'And now, Hattie,

I wish to give *you* something, by way of a thank you.'

'I don't need anything,' said Hattie. 'Really. I've had an amazing time and I'm just glad I could help you.' But Mith Ickle was already busy puffing out another small burst of fire.

As the flames and smoke cleared, Hattie saw something fall with a small *chink* to the cave floor by her feet. Picking it up gently, she saw it was a small, silver dragon charm, about the same size as her star charm. Hattie immediately clipped it to her bracelet and gave Mith Ickle a careful hug, avoiding her still-smoking, and now fire-filled, snout.

As she reluctantly pulled away, a thought occurred to Hattie, and she didn't feel quite so happy any more.

'I guess that means you'll be back off to your dragon friends in Bellua now, Mith,' she said sadly. 'Thank you for helping me out on my first visit. I'm going to miss you very much, you know.' Hattie wiped away the tears that had quickly filled her eyes as she prepared to wave goodbye.

But, to Hattie's surprise, Mith Ickle stayed right where she was and didn't look very ready to go anywhere.

'I won't leave you forever, Hattie,' she sang. 'You are sure to find yourself in the Kingdom of Bellua again if King Ivar steals the magical power of another unfortunate creature. And, when you do, you can be certain I'll be here to guide you. There can be dangers in Bellua, and a creature that knows the kingdom as I do could be a great help to a Guardian of little experience, such as you.'

Mith Ickle fluttered over and wrapped herself round Hattie's shoulders. Hattie couldn't help thinking that Mith Ickle would be there for her as a friend as much as a guide and that the little dragon was as fond of her new Guardian as Hattie was of her first magical patient.

Even though she knew that she'd see Mith Ickle again, Hattie still felt a little sad at leaving her new friend.

'I suppose I really ought to get back to my

own world now,' she said, resting her chin gloomily on her folded arms.

'I will see you soon, Hattie,' reassured the little dragon, hopping on to the table and nudging her affectionately on one cheek.

'Try not to get into any trouble while I'm away!' teased Hattie, as she reached for the sparkly vet's bag and hesitantly peered inside. For the second time that day, she found herself tumbling down, down and down . . .

Best Friends Forever ✦

Hattie landed on her bed with a bounce. She quickly opened her eyes and saw that her room was just as she'd left it. A DVD was still whirring in the player, and the brown paper with the strange stamp and writing on it was crumpled on the floor. Next to her, the vet's bag lay locked shut, no longer silver and sparkly but back to its dull brown leather. Had she imagined it all? The cave, Mith Ickle and the magical Kingdom of Bellua?

Then Hattie looked down at her wrist and saw both the star and the dragon charm hanging from her bracelet. Bellua *was* real. Hattie knew she really had been there.

It was only when Hattie went on to think about everything else she had seen in Bellua that she realized how long she must have been away from her room. There were the unicorns and the trolls, Immie and the naughty fairies, meadows and forests, and volcanoes and mountains . . .

Mum and Dad must have been back for hours, she thought, jumping to her feet. *They'll be wondering where on earth I've been! I bet even Peter's worried!*

Hattie ran out of her room and on to the landing, peering over the banisters to the hall below. Just at that moment, the front door

swung open and in swept Hattie's mum and dad, dumping coats and bags as the door slammed shut behind them.

'Hattie, we're back!' Mum called up the stairs as she started to climb them and head towards Hattie's bedroom. 'It's nearly lunchtime, you know. Have you been lazing in your room all this time? I'd expect that of your brother, but not you, Hattie!'

Nearly lunchtime? thought Hattie, more than a little confused. It was almost lunchtime when she'd left. Surely she'd been in the cave and Bellua for the best part of a day? She couldn't believe it!

Glancing at the bracelet again, something

began to make sense to Hattie. She was now sure of two things. Firstly, she was definitely the Guardian of the magical Kingdom of Bellua. Secondly, and luckily, no time had passed in the real world since she'd first tumbled into the cave. As Uncle B had done before her, Hattie decided this was a secret that she would keep to herself forever – or at least until the next Guardian came along – and so she figured that telling her mum a little fib wasn't really so bad.

'Yep, Mum,' she said. 'I've just been hanging out in my room, watching a couple of DVDs Chloe lent me.'

As she mentioned her friend's name, Hattie remembered how cross she had been with

Chloe earlier, and what a terrible birthday morning she'd had, and how her parents hadn't even mentioned it . . . but, before she could open her mouth to say anything else, her mum began guiding her down the stairs.

'I think there's something in the lounge you might want to see,' Mum said, as she followed Hattie. A small flicker of hope crossed Hattie's mind. Maybe there *would* be a birthday present for her at least, or perhaps a cake? She hurried towards the closed living-room door and turned the handle.

'*SURPRISE!!!*'

Hattie couldn't believe it! Lined up on both sides of the fireplace were Dad, Peter,

Chloe and all her friends from school, holding presents wrapped in different kinds of animal wrapping paper. Balloons were tied in bunches around the room, and above the fireplace hung a long banner saying, *HAPPY BIRTHDAY, HATTIE!* When Hattie looked at the writing on the banner, she knew at once that it was Chloe's – and that her friend must have spent ages making it.

Before Hattie could say anything more than 'Wow!' everyone broke into a loud chorus of 'Happy Birthday' as Mum appeared with a cat-shaped birthday cake, blazing with ten sparkly candles.

'Thank you, everyone!' cried Hattie as she

blew the candles out with a puff that she thought even Mith Ickle would have been proud of. 'This is the best birthday EVER!'

Thinking of Mith Ickle brought a smile to Hattie's face as she remembered how pleased she was to have helped her first magical creature. She thought too of how Mith Ickle had healed her injured hand, then saved her from the frozen Winter Mountains when Hattie feared she would be left there all alone. Hattie was sure she had a true friend in Mith Ickle – and now she knew how silly she had been to think that Chloe, her best friend in all the world, had forgotten her birthday.

'So you weren't at your cousin's after all!'

laughed Hattie, turning towards Chloe and giving her a big hug. 'Your mum's a pretty good actress, you know. She had me totally fooled!'

'As if,' replied Chloe. 'I'd never miss your birthday in a million years! You're my best friend ever, Hattie.'

Hattie knew Chloe was right – they really were best friends. But hadn't she used the words 'ex-best friend' earlier that day?

Mumbling something about needing to get a drink, Hattie dashed out of the living room and into the kitchen. There on the table was Mum's pile of letters, still waiting to be posted.

Hattie grabbed the tear-stained envelope that lay on top. She was full of relief that

Mum hadn't posted it yet. Turning red with shame, she tore both the envelope and letter into small pieces and pushed them deep into the kitchen bin. Then she headed back to the living room, where a huge pile of presents now lay on the coffee table ready to be opened.

'Mine first!' called Chloe, holding out a card that read:

To Hattie with lots and lots of love from
Chloe, your best friend forever xxx

And then she handed Hattie a soft and squidgy parcel wrapped in silver paper.

With pink dragons all over it . . .

In bed that night, after Chloe had fallen asleep, Hattie could hardly believe what an eventful tenth birthday she'd had. After such a terrible start, she certainly hadn't expected to find herself exploring a fantastical land, protecting magical creatures from an evil Imp King *and* enjoying the best surprise party ever.

As her eyes grew heavy and sleep beckoned, she felt her tummy stir with butterflies. *I just hope King Ivar doesn't put any more creatures in danger – but I will help them if he does.* Hattie touched the delicate charms on her bracelet and couldn't help thinking that perhaps another adventure was only round the corner.

Find out more about

Hattie B

Hair – jet black with an unusual white streak. She may be teased about this streak, but it has magic running through it!

Birthmark – a tiny but perfect star on Hattie's right cheek. Stars feature many times in the magical Kingdom of Bellua ...

Charm bracelet – the most gorgeous birthday gift Hattie's ever received. After her adventure with Mith Ickle, she has a little dragon charm to go with her tiny crystal star!

Loves animals – every single one! From puppies and ponies to the unicorns, dragons and many, many more creatures in Bellua!

Best friend – Chloe Pickles. Always there for each other, they've been friends FOREVER.

Dreams of being a vet ... whether in this world like her mum and dad or in Bellua to all the mythical creatures. Who knows? Hopefully both!

Find out what happens next in

The Unicorn's Horn

Hattie B returns to the Kingdom of Bellua
where wicked King Ivar has taken the magic
from a unicorn's horn!

Only Hattie can make the special medicine
the unicorn needs — can she find the
ingredients before it's too late?

www.worldofhattieb.com

Hattie's Trail

Which path must Hattie follow to reach the Rumbling Volcano?

A

B

C

Hattie B
Magical Vet

Find out more about
Hattie B
and the creatures
from the
Kingdom of
Bellua

by visiting

www.worldofhattieb.com